One Winter's Night

ONE WINTER'S NIGHT

By JOHN HERMAN   Illustrated by LEO AND DIANE DILLON

PHILOMEL BOOKS

Martha was lost.

It was bitter cold, snow was beginning to fall. It was too late in the year for a young cow to be out alone, especially when she was pregnant.

The snow hissed like sand across the frozen fields. It beat against Martha's sides. It blew in squalls out of the darkened air.

Martha's coat had grown in shaggy and thick against the winter, but she shivered anyway. She knew her time was near. She had to find her way back to warmth and safety.

Then slowly the clouds blew off. The snow stopped. Stars appeared in the sky. A single star burned brightly on the eastern horizon. And Martha followed it, her bell chiming on the cold wind, dong dong.

She passed three deer foraging at the edge of the forest. She passed a fox, its red coat a scarlet whisk against the snow. Slowly Martha crossed the fields, the clear round O of her bell a small sigh in the wind, dong dong.

Now Martha had found a path through the stubble. She had to be
careful not to slip on the frozen mud. Below her she saw a farm. She
thought of a barn. The warmth of a manger. The sound of people.

But as Martha descended the hill she was puzzled. She saw no dog. No light from windows. No smoke from chimneys. She heard only the whistle of wind, the slap of a loose porch door.

Martha stood in the front yard and lowed at the empty house, but no one answered. An upturned pail lay frozen by the steps. She walked to the barn but the door was closed. She pushed against it with her nose. But no one was there to help.

Martha stepped over the frozen wagon ruts, and her bell made a hollow sound in the wind, dong dong. Night had come, the wind keened in the frozen branches. The star she followed burned brighter than the others, like a single jet of flame above the horizon.

Martha could see the tracks of wild animals in the frozen snow. Squirrels, raccoons, the small birds of the air. But nowhere the familiar prints of farm animals. It was as if the earth had been abandoned.

She saw a small shed at the end of the field. It stood on the crest of a
hill. Snow glittered on the black branches around the shelter. The light
from the star gleamed like silver on the frozen white.

Martha pushed with her nose against the door of the shed. She smelled the familiar odor of warmth and hay.

A light burned. A donkey stirred in a stall. Martha smelled the odor of humans. She knew they would help her and her baby.

"Who's there?" A man rose from where he had been sitting in the hay next to a young woman. He wore a full beard and a woolen coat.

"Look." The man frowned. "A young cow. And she's pregnant—just like you."

"Go to her," the young woman said. Her hair was dark, and she looked at the man out of large dark eyes. She was dressed simply, with a scarf over her head against the cold. But even in the hay she was radiant.

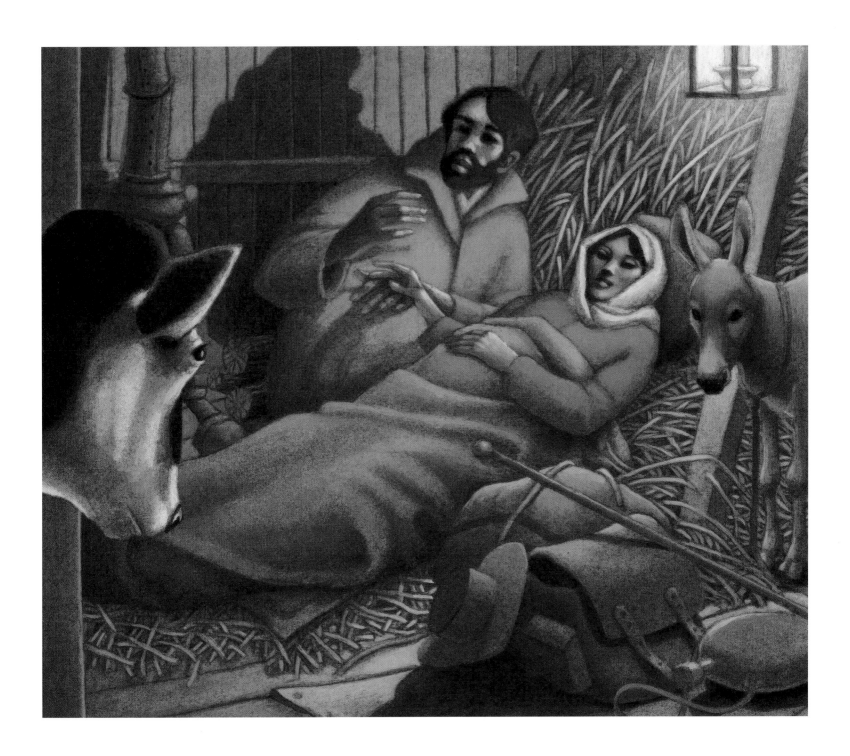

"What are you doing out alone on a night like this?" the man said, approaching Martha. "And ready to give birth. Couldn't you find anyplace else to go?"

He stroked her, leading her forward as he spoke. Her bell made a pleasant swaying sound as she walked, dong dong.

The man led Martha into the space by the donkey. He brought her hay and settled her down. "Out alone in the cold night, just like us."

Martha munched the hay, inhaling the pleasant smell of the donkey. The sound of the man's voice reassured her.

The cold blew into the stall. Through the open window Martha saw the night. She saw the snow. She saw the glitter of the distant star.

Now Martha felt the heavy pang of birth. She opened her mouth and lowed. She had never given birth before, and she was afraid.

"There, there," the man said as he stroked her. "There is nothing to fear. Everything will be all right."

Martha's eyes rolled, but the words of the man comforted her.

"Joseph!" the young woman called from where she lay by the manger. "Come if you can. Come quick!"

Outside the wind shook the trees. The forest moaned. The branches gave a cracking sound like the report of a gun. The star in the East gleamed in the ragged branches of the pines.

In the shed Martha panted long and hard.

All was blackness. Darkest night. The winds fell from the four corners and shook the earth. Only the icy fire of the stars, distant and brilliant, kept watch in the darkness.

And then finally there was a small cry.

"It is over," the woman's voice said.

"Yes," the man said. "And just beginning."

Martha lowed.

"Goodness!" he exclaimed. "The young cow!"

The man hurried to the stall. Martha lay exhausted, her sides still panting. And beside her, just beginning to stand on spindly legs—a beautiful calf.

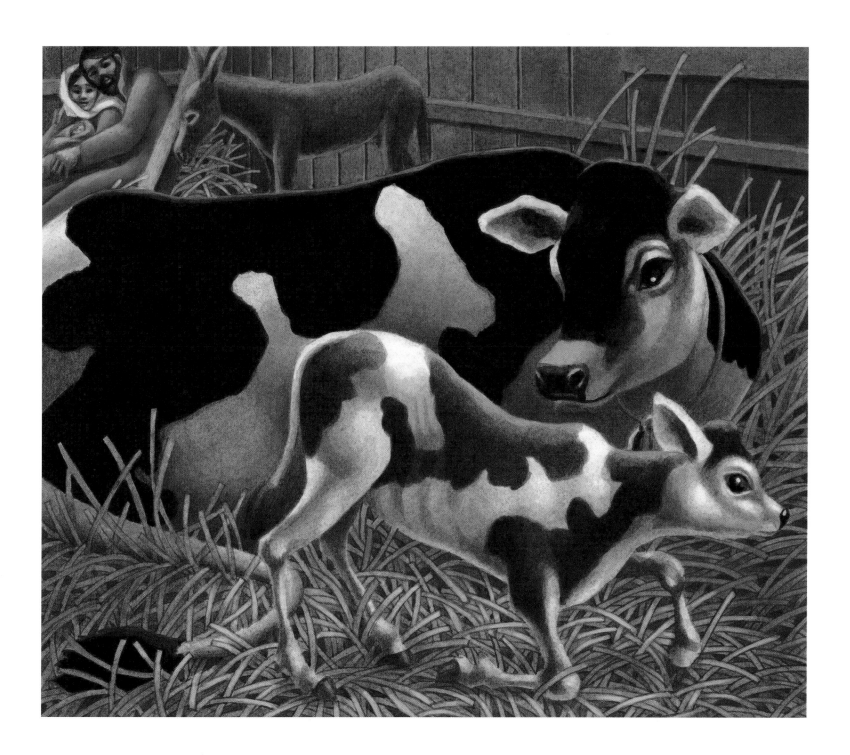

"Is she all right?" the woman called from where she lay with her son.

"She's fine," the man answered.

Martha was tired, but her baby was butting against her, already searching for milk. She licked the calf with her large rough tongue.

The man paused by the open window. Outside the sky was black but the stars still burned in the heavens. The light from the eastern star glowed on the fallen snow.

"Well, now, two glorious babies on one winter's night," the man said. And he smiled at Mary beside him.

Patricia Lee Gauch, editor

Text copyright © 2003 by John Herman.
Illustrations copyright © 2003 by Leo and Diane Dillon.
All rights reserved. This book, or parts thereof, may not be reproduced in any form
without permission in writing from the publisher,
PHILOMEL BOOKS,
a division of Penguin Putnam Books for Young Readers,
345 Hudson Street, New York, NY 10014.
Philomel Books, Reg. U.S. Pat. & Tm. Off. The scanning, uploading and distribution of this book
via the Internet or via any other means without the permission of the publisher is illegal and punishable by law.
Please purchase only authorized electronic editions, and do not participate in or encourage electronic piracy of
copyrighted materials. Your support of the author's rights is appreciated.
Published simultaneously in Canada.
Printed in the United States of America.

Book design by Semadar Megged.   The text is set in 17-point Horley Old Style.
The art was rendered in watercolor and pastel on Arches hotpress watercolor paper.

Library of Congress Cataloging-in-Publication Data

Herman, John, date.
One winter's night / by John Herman ; illustrated by Leo and Diane Dillon.   p. cm.
Summary: A lonely cow about to give birth on a cold winter's night finds shelter in a deserted shed
with a man and a woman who are also having a baby. [1. Cows—Fiction. 2. Birth—Fiction.
3. Jesus Christ—Nativity—Fiction.] I. Dillon, Leo, ill. II. Dillon, Diane, ill. III. Title.
PZ7.H41353 On 2003 [E]—dc21 2002015408
ISBN 0-399-23418-7
1 3 5 7 9 10 8 6 4 2
First Impression